THE WALRUS AND THE CARIBOU

PUBLISHER'S NOTE:

This book is based on an Inuit traditional story. Versions of this story can be found across the Inuit North. The story you are about to read is a creative retelling of this original story.

Published by Inhabit Media Inc. · www.inhabitmedia.com
Inhabit Media Inc. (Iqaluit) P.O. Box 11125, Iqaluit, Nunavut, X0A 1H0
(Toronto) 191 Eglinton Avenue East, Suite 310, Toronto, Ontario, M4P 1K1

Design and layout copyright ©2019 Inhabit Media Inc.
Text copyright ©2019 Maika Harper
Illustrations by Marcus Cutler copyright ©2019 Inhabit Media Inc.

Editors: Neil Christopher and Kelly Ward
Art Director: Danny Christopher
Designer: Astrid Arijanto
Cultural Advisor: Roselynn Akulukjuk

We acknowledge the support of the Canada Council for the Arts for our publishing program. This project has been made possible in part by the Government of Canada.

ISBN: 978-1-77227-256-7

Library and Archives Canada Cataloguing in Publication

Title: The walrus and the caribou / by Maika Harper ; illustrated by Marcus Cutler.
Names: Harper, Maika, 1986- author. | Cutler, Marcus, 1978- illustrator.
Identifiers: Canadiana 20190190957 | ISBN 9781772272567 (hardcover)
Classification: LCC PS8615.A7458565 W35 2019 | DDC jC813/.6-dc23

Printed in Canada

THE WALRUS AND THE CARIBOU

BY MAIKA HARPER

ILLUSTRATED BY MARCUS CUTLER

INTRODUCTION

Versions of this story can be found across the Arctic, from the Labrador Inuit all the way to Alaska. It focuses on the power of willing intentions into creation. I have loved learning traditional stories since childhood and was so lucky to have great storytellers in my family and in my community of Iqaluit, Nunavut. My favourite memories are of camping on the land and telling stories in the tent. To this day that is still my favourite place to hear and tell stories. The traditional origin stories of Inuit are plentiful and powerful and always leave you learning something new. I hope this book does just that.

-MAIKA HARPER

A long time ago, when the world was taking shape, a little woman began breathing life into the world. Her name was Guk.

How does an animal take shape? she thought. Where does the head go? What goes on the head? Ears? Whiskers? A snout?

First came the walrus.
Breathing in. Breathing out.
Guk created the walrus from her sealskin parka.

Whiskers and wrinkles and funny dancing flippers.
The walrus had huge antlers, too!

Every time it swam, it would
overturn the kayaks in the water.
The antlers were too big.
The hunters were upset.

Once again, Guk breathed in, she breathed out. Then she created the caribou from her sealskin pants.

Big hooves and hair everywhere.
A large snout and tusks, too!

Every time it saw a hunter, the caribou
would charge him with its tusks, creating
much trouble on the land.
The tusks were too big.
The hunters were, again, upset.

What would happen if the walrus and the caribou traded different parts of their bodies? Guk thought.

Guk called, "Qaigissik, qaigissik. Come, come," to the walrus and the caribou.

Pulling the tusks out of the caribou's mouth, she gave them to the walrus. Then she pulled the antlers from the walrus's head and gave them to the caribou.

THERE!

Remembering the trouble the caribou had caused, she called, "Qaigit, qaigit. Come, come."

As punishment for hurting the hunters, she kicked its forehead flat, and its eyes bulged.

"For being so rude, you will stay far away inland!" she scolded.

Ever since, whenever a caribou smells a human,
it is afraid.

If your intentions had the power of creation, what animal would you make? Would it have feathers? Or a big furry tail? Imagine the possibilities!

MAIKA HARPER is a Canadian actress and model born and raised in the Arctic. She briefly studied classical theatre in the BFA program at the University of Windsor before starring in APTN's hit dramatic comedy *Mohawk Girls* as Anna. She has also made appearances on *Kim's Convenience*, and most recently on *Burden of Truth*. Her theatrical debut was as an alternate in *Treasure Island* at the 2017 Stratford Festival, and her film debut will be in *The Education of Fredrick Fitzell* in 2019. In her spare time, she advocates for mental health awareness and mentors youth in Canada with Youth Fusion.

MARCUS CUTLER is a both a children's illustrator and an occasional climber of rocks. He lives and works in Windsor, Ontario, with his wife and two daughters.

GLOSSARY

Notes on Inuktitut Pronunciation

There are some sounds in Inuktitut that may be unfamiliar to English speakers. The pronunciations below convey those sounds in the following ways:

- Capitalized letters denote the emphasis.
- q is an "uvular" sound, a sound that comes from the very back of the throat. This is distinct from the sound for k, which is the same as a typical English "k" sound.

qaigissik qai-GIS-sik Come (when referring to two individuals)

qaigit QAI-git Come (when referring to one individual)

For more Inuktitut language resources, including audio recordings of the terms found in this book, please visit inhabitmedia.com/inuitnipingit.

INHABIT MEDIA

IQALUIT • TORONTO